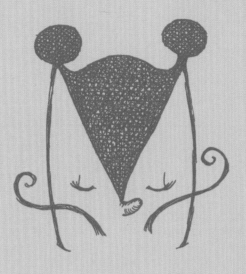

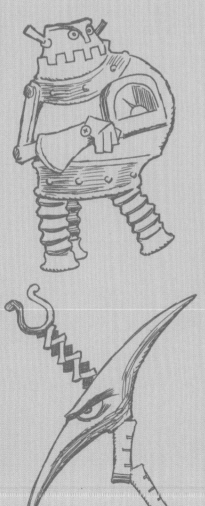

G is for One Gzonk!

AN ALPHA-NUMBER-BET BOOK

by TINY DiTERLOONEY

(a.k.a. Tony DiTerlizzi)

SIMON & SCHUSTER BOOKS for YOUNG READERS

NEW YORK OZ LONDON TORONTO NEVERLAND SYDNEY

Tiny would like to thank Joey B, Markael, John, Holly, EGV, Jane, and Heidi.

Kevin, thanks for making it look like I can really rhyme well,

and thank you, Ang, for my new nickname.

SIMON & SCHUSTER BOOKS FOR YOUNG READERS

An imprint of Simon & Schuster Children's Publishing Division

1230 Avenue of the Americas, New York, New York 10020

Copyright © 2006 Tony DiTerlizzi

All rights reserved, including the right of reproduction in whole or in part in any form.

SIMON & SCHUSTER BOOKS FOR YOUNG READERS is a trademark of Simon & Schuster, Inc.

Book design by Tony DiTerlizzi and Michael Nelson

The text for this book is set in Century Schoolbook.

The pen-and-ink illustrations of the creachlings were colored digitally in an effort

to emulate the spot-printing coloration used in picture books of the 1940s and 1950s.

Tiny and the Woos were painted in Holbein acryla gouache and detailed with Berol prismacolor pencils.

Manufactured in China

2 4 6 8 10 9 7 5 3 1

CIP data for this book is available from the Library of Congress.

ISBN-13: 978-0-689-85290-9

ISBN-10: 0-689-85290-8

first edition

In memory of Good Doctor Ted,
his pantone pantomime
and surgical precision
with picture, wit, and rhyme,

and the Jolly Englishman-
with glasses, beard, and hat-
who always made me smile with his
"Owl and Pussy-cat."

-T. D

Hello! And welcome to my book!
A book thought up by me.
I am the author and artist
(as soon you'll plainly see)

of this alphabet of creachlings!
A twenty-six-letter menagerie!
But I must confess,
as you may have guessed,
it won't teach you A B C.

So say good-bye to boring books
where "bears can bounce a ball,"
and turn the page;
I've set the stage,
and nothing makes sense at all.

Aa

A is for an **Angry Ack**.
He eats your dirty clothes.
His favorite snack is stinky socks
with jam packed in the toes.

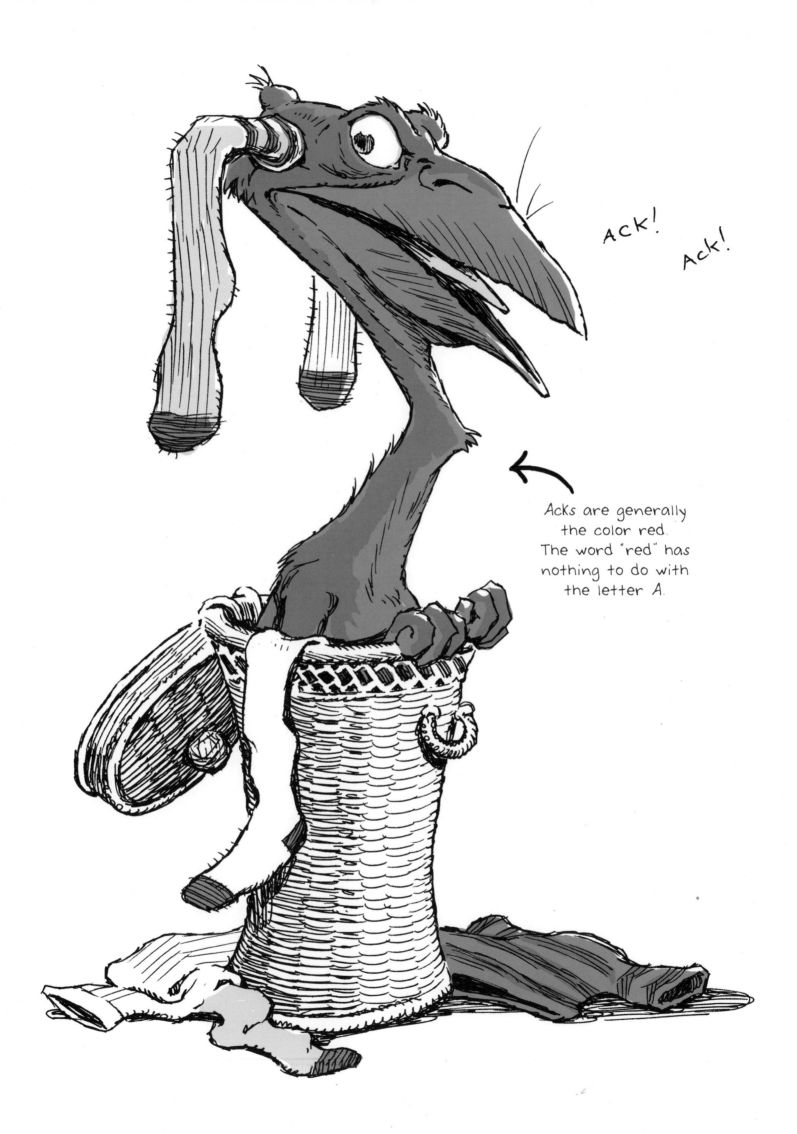

And grabbing goodies off the floor,
the snooping **Bloobytack**
puts every object he can find
upon his sticky back.

A toy car,
a vase,
a fork,
a watch once owned by me.
And, as you know, not one of these
begins with letter **B**.

Paintbrush begins
with the letter P.

Cc

The **Cootie-Noodle** (letter **C**)
has gotta dance and sing.
Too bad she has a voice so high,
you cannot hear a thing.

Cootie-Noodle
loves pink.
It's her
favoritist color
in the world.

I can't even think of a fruit that begins with the letter D.

Dd

The **Dinkalicious Dinky**
eats bananas from a tin
early each and every morning
doing yoga on a pin!

Ee

The E on his chest is for EVIL!

E is for an **Evil Eeog**,
with hateful horrid breath,
and if you sniff a little whiff,
you may be faced with death!

These are dead flies.
Yes, his breath is *that* bad!

Ff

Eeog's stinky breath reeked onto this page.

And here we see the frantic
Fly-Swatting Footzey-Foo.
He never ever hits his mark. . . .
Wait!
Who the heck are you?

Ff

I AM ONESIE. I AM TWOSIE.
WE ARE TEEDLE-WEENIE WOO!
YOU NEVER SEE JUST 1 OF US.
THERE MUST AT LEAST BE 2.

AND IF YOU DO SEE 2 OF US,
THEN SOON THERE WILL BE 3. . . .

Hold on! This is no counting book!
'Cause that's not A B C.
Go back to where you came from.
Wherever that may be.

Gg

Now, **G** is for the **Grand Gzonk**,
who everybody knows
can take the oddest things and
balance them upon his nose!

Looks like a GOLDFISH,
but it is a PIRANHA,
so no G's here.

You could say he is GREEN,
but I say he is AVOCADO.

Okay, he's wearing a HAT.
But he's wearing a BOWTIE, too.
And there are no H's in BOWTIE.

Here's a **Hungry Hoofle-Foofle** . . .

Ii

. . . and Ack's twin brother, **Ick**.
He sneezes, wheezes, snorts, and drips,
because he's always sick.

If this were a normal alphabet book, I'd say he has INDIGESTION. But it looks like a COLD to me.

Jammy Jelly Jello-melly
wears pj's all day.
While pouring cups of hot grape juice,
he makes PB&J!

Kk

Observe the one-eyed **Krigglebink** slurp catsup through a straw. . . .

And a **Large Licky Lickins**—
the biggest thing I ever saw!

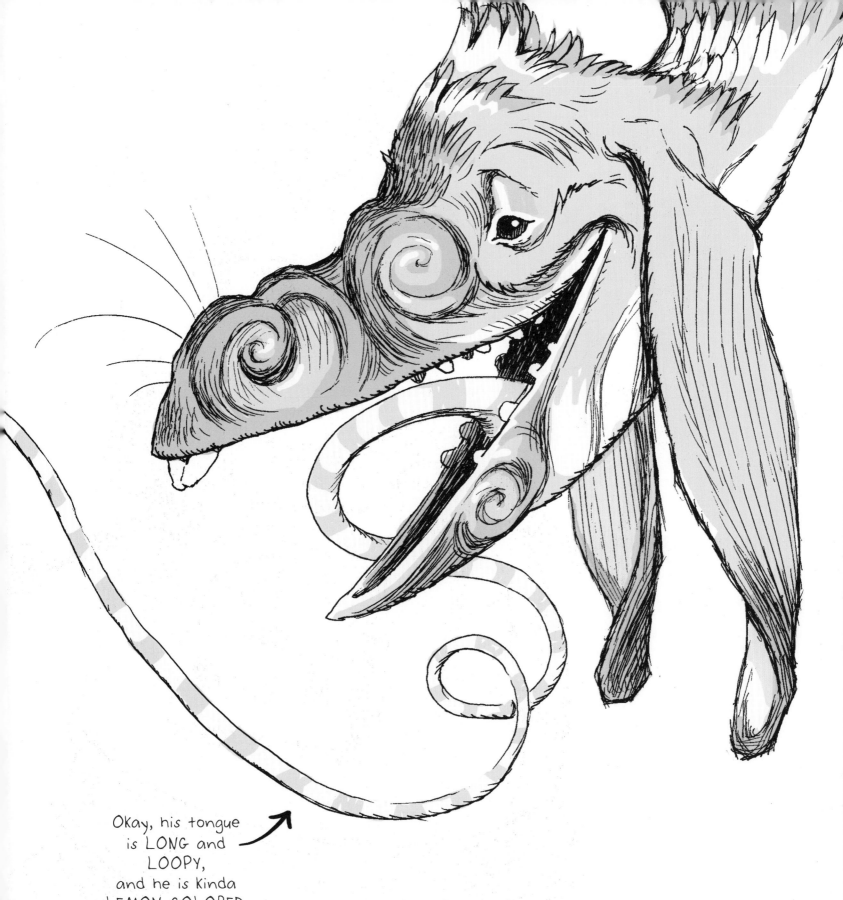

Okay, his tongue
is LONG and
LOOPY,
and he is kinda
LEMON-COLORED.

Rr

R STANDS FOR **RAVENOUS ROTOID**,
WITH **60** SCREWS INSIDE HIS HEAD. . . .

No. R doesn't come after L, you Woo.
It comes after Q instead.

Mm

Barbell.
(See letter B.)

Behold!
The
**Mighty
Mee-yighty . . .**

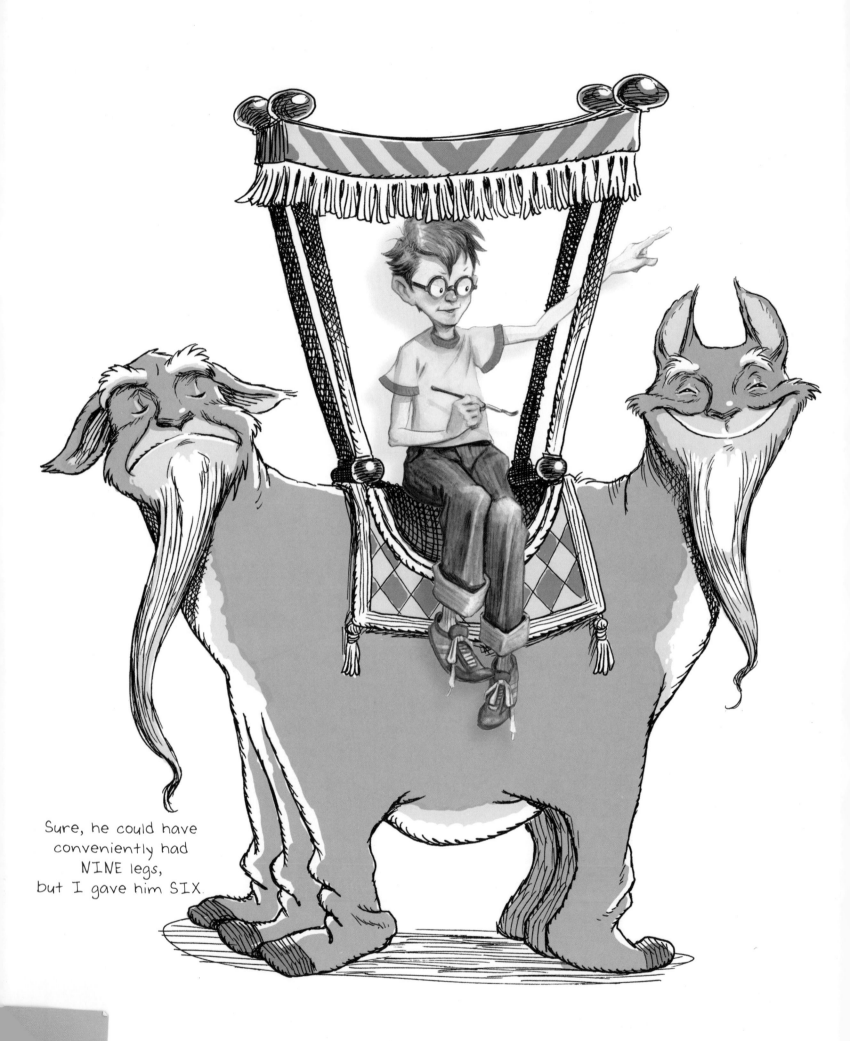

Sure, he could have conveniently had NINE legs, but I gave him SIX.

. . . and the **Neenel-Nonnel,** too.

I THINK THIS GUY SHOULD HAVE **4** LEGS.

OR NOTHING LESS THAN **2**.

Onesie! Twosie! Cut it out!
This ain't the place for you!

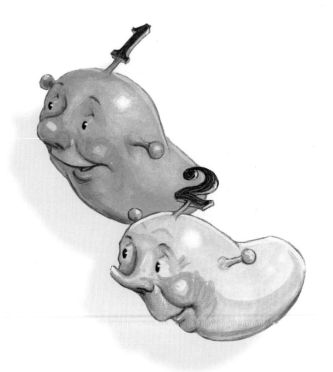

Oo

Make way for the zoomy **Orange Oomy,**

WEIGHING IN AT **2.5** LITERS.

Threesie, you're ruining letter **O.**

BUT SHE JUST RAN **39** METERS!

Pp

Yeah, yeah, POTTY begins with the letter P, but I'm not a little baby.

Sure it's paper, but it's TOILET paper.

Pink Peepee-Weepkins

sleeps soundly on the loo. . . .

THERE'S **7** STARS UPON HIS CAP.

THAT'S IT! I've HAD it with you!

Count for me, smarty, the hairs on his head.
Divide that by how many ears,
multiply that by the stripes on his tongue,
and subtract his age in dog years.

Pp

Wow . . . that is astounding.
Your adding skills are great.

Perhaps it would not be so bad
to count the A B C.
Let's try it together.
You take the next letter,
the one that comes right after P.

Your average, everyday
alphabet book would use
the old standby:
a QUAIL for Q.
Not in this book, mister.

CRAZY CUTESIE **QUEASY QUAPP**
IS ALLERGIC TO HER NAPS,
EVEN AFTER PADDLING
90 SPLISHY-SPLASHY LAPS.

I think I can work with you digits.
In fact, it might just be nifty
to keep counting our letters
and splitting them each fifty-fifty.

Rrr! goes the **Ravenous Rotoid**
WITH **60** SCREWS INSIDE HIS HEAD.
AND **1** CASE OF BLISTERING HEARTBURN
from eating big hunks of hot lead!

Aa

A IS FOR AN **ANGRY ACK**.

HE EATS **8** POUNDS OF CLOTHES.

Wait! We did "A" a while ago,
as everyone here knows.

BUT WE MISSED THE VERY BEGINNING.

YES, WE WANT TO COUNT FROM THE START!

Twosie! Threesie! Stop it, now!
You're tearing my book apart.

The **Striped and Squirty Swizzle-Whizzle**
yells and spits and spurts.
HE HAS YELLED **6** TIMES TODAY,
and now my eardrums hurt!

1. WHEN HE WAS ANGRY.
2. WHEN HE WAS BORED.
3. WHEN HE WAS HAPPY.

And when he was ignored.

He yelled at a ham sandwich *and*
the Hoofle-Foofle's tail.
He yelled so much,
his voice gave up,
and jumped into a pail.

Tt

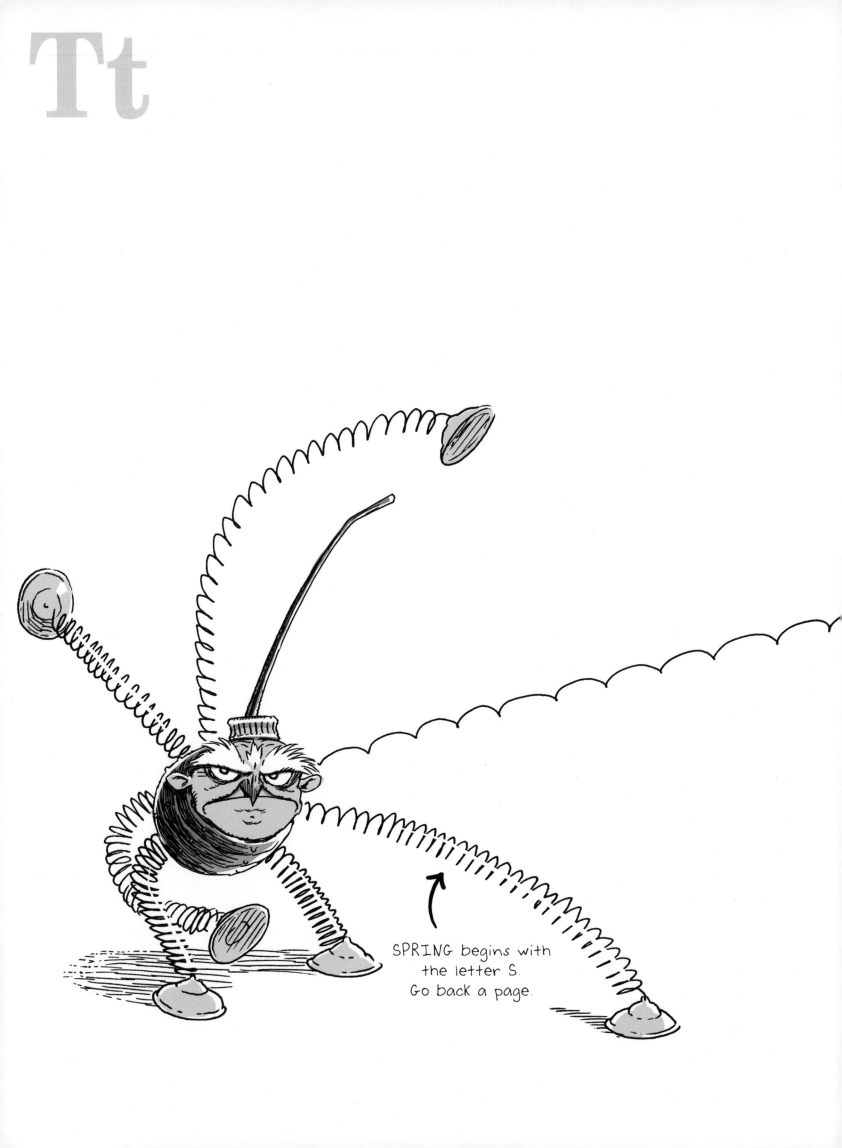

SPRING begins with the letter S. Go back a page.

T is the **Teensy Teety-Tee**,
WITH **7** LEGS IN ALL,
AND **7** STICKY SUCTION CUPS
to climb right up the wall.

Onesie, Twosie, wait a sec!
This just came to me.
We can count, and count some more,
after letter Z.

Uu

The **Uggle-Unk**, with floating hands,
plays guitar upside down!
THERE ARE **3** STRIPES IN HIS UNDERWEAR.
Thank goodness, none are brown.

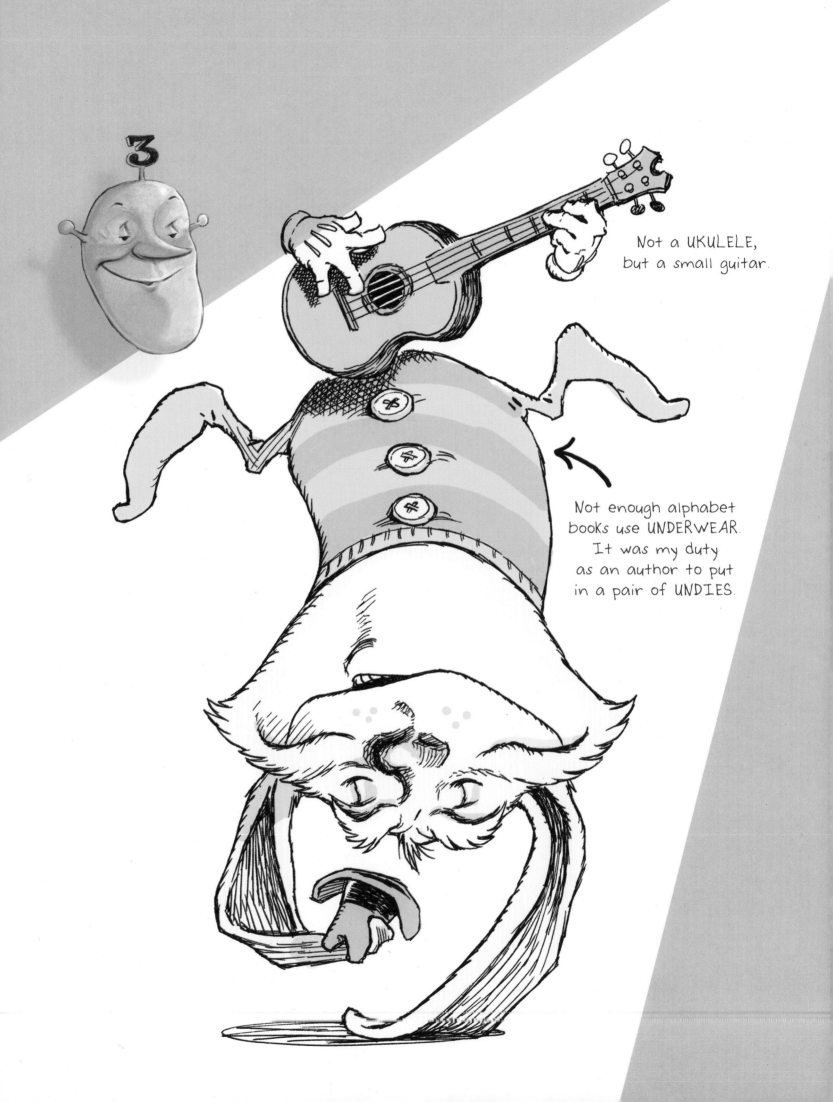

Not a UKULELE,
but a small guitar.

Not enough alphabet
books use UNDERWEAR.
It was my duty
as an author to put
in a pair of UNDIES.

3

Vv

Careful, Teedle-Weenie Woo.
Let's hurry on our way.
The **Vicious, Vile, and Venomous Vritt**
did not come here to play.

Beware! He is also VIOLET and VULGAR!

Ww

Well, here we are at **W**—
with the **Whirly Whirleroo**.
And hold on. . . . Am I counting right?
Do I see two more Woo?

I can't stand
WILD and WACKY
(common "W" words
in alphabet books),
so I didn't use them.

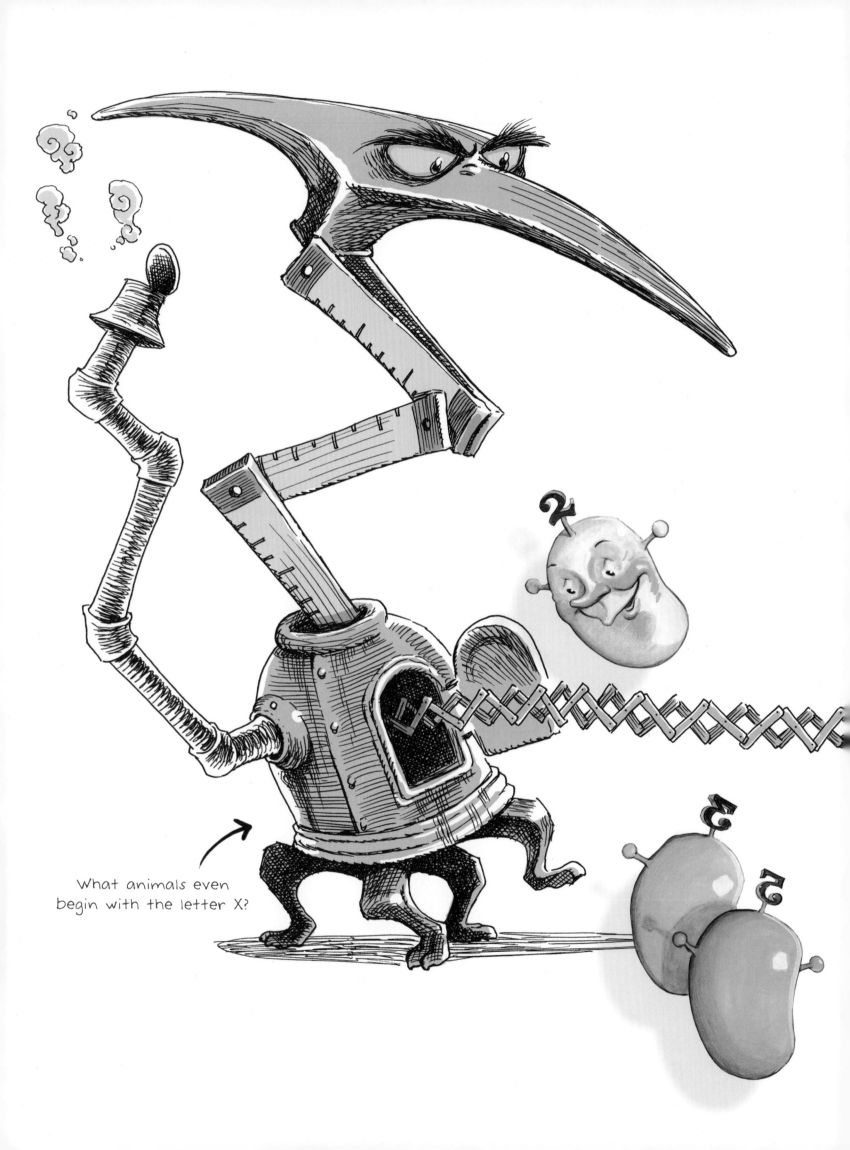

What animals even begin with the letter X?

X STANDS FOR THE NUMBER **10**,
SO NOW THERE ARE **10** WOO!
Or **X** could be this **Xirzle**, who
is trying to cook my shoe!

HIS CROOKED NECK IS **3** FEET LONG.
HIS LEGS, THEY NUMBER **4**.
HIS ARM EXTENDS **500** YARDS
FROM **1** BIG METAL DOOR.

We are finding stuff to count.
So much we cannot stop.
Just like the **Yellow Yummel-Yum**,
who counts each single hop.

HE HOPS **8** MILLION HOPS TO WORK,

9 ZILLION TO THE STORE.

Then he hops back home again
because his hopper's sore.

I suppose this fella could be
YELPING because of his sore
hopper, but Yummel-Yums don't
yelp; they're too dignified.

Zibble Zooks
love reading dictionaries.
They use real "Z" words
like ZERBLE and
ZACROTOGRAPHY, not
ZEBRA and ZOO.

The letter **Z** will always be
the **Zanderiffic Zibble Zook**,
the final fancy entry in
this alpha-bet-a-licious book.

With one and twenty consonants
plus A, E, I, O, U—
that's twenty-six creachlings in all!
My masterpiece is through!

Wow! This book of A B C
has been a world of fun.
Now let me do a counting book.
I'll start with number 1.

So all you Woo race up ahead
and find your proper place.
And when I say your number,
then you'll know to show your face.

1 orange Woo,
sitting all alone,
calls up another Woo
on the telephone.
"Hey you, Woo,
what do you wanna do?"
He hopped over
and then there were **2**.

ACK
ACK